Zen Pig

Book 2

The Wonder We Are

written by:

mark brown

illustrated by:

amy lynn larwig

Spread the love with...
#ZenPig

Dedicated to Amy, who has access to some of my Zen-less moments, yet still supports me.

Thank you.

Granted the gift
Of the sun's first light,
Zen Pig sits with a tree
Enjoying the sight.

Passers-by stop
Amidst a morning stroll
To curiously ask, "What's Zen Pig up to
On that green, grassy knoll?"

One said to the other,
"I'm not quite sure."
The other looked excited
And said, "Let's find out more."

"Excuse us, Zen Pig.
Please tell us what you see,
Because to us it appears
To be just a regular old tree."

"Ah," Zen Pig said,
A small smile on his face.
"The tree is just the beginning,
There's much more to embrace.

When I look at this tree
I see every drop of rain,
Every ray of sunlight,
Every bird it will sustain.

Within a glass of water,
There lies a cloud in the sky.
Within every piece of toast,
A farmer on which it relies.

Every plant and every being
Are all intertwined.
The well-being of all
We must bear in mind.

The whole of nature
Is more than it appears.
We must look closely
And keep our minds clear,

Then we will see
The wonder we are;
Our great connection
Even with the stars.

No matter what you see,
Take the time to look close
And you'll be marveled and amazed
By what it will show."

Namaste.

("The light in me loves the light in you.")

Name: _____

Age: _____ Date: _____

Zen Pig's Question:

What is one thing in nature YOU are grateful for?

_____

_____

_____

_____